MacCrimmon's Sweetheart

Air adapted from the pibroch   Words by Gerry & George Armstrong

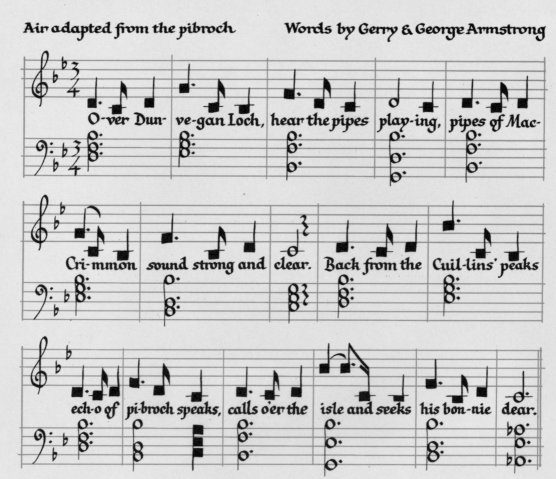

O-ver Dun- ve-gan Loch, hear the pipes play-ing, pipes of Mac-Cri-mmon sound strong and clear. Back from the Cuil-lins' peaks ech-o of pi-broch speaks, calls o'er the isle and seeks his bon-nie dear.

Bonnie the isle, with its plaidie of heather,
Ribboned with sparkling, silvery streams;
Beauty of bird on wing, mystery of fairy ring,
Murmur of sea waves sing, filling my dreams.

Dunvegan Loch

🏰 Dunvegan Castle

Isle of Skye

Cuillin Hills

The Magic Bagpipe

The MAGIC BAGPIPE

By Gerry and George Armstrong

ALBERT WHITMAN & COMPANY · Chicago

© 1964 by Albert Whitman & Company, Chicago. L.C. Catalog Card 64-7717
Published simultaneously in Canada by George J. McLeod, Ltd., Toronto
Lithographed in the United States of America

Foreword

The greatest pipers in Scottish history and legend were the MacCrimmons of Skye. For about three hundred years they held the position of hereditary pipers to the MacLeods of Dunvegan.

The MacCrimmons founded a school of piping on the Isle of Skye which offered a course of from six to twelve years. No piper's training was considered complete until he had studied under these master pipers.

According to legend, the MacCrimmons received their gift of piping from the fairies.

G.A.

A Bagpipe Practice Chanter

A Highland Bagpipe
of the 15th Century

ONCE UPON A TIME, long ago, there was a young boy named Donald MacCrimmon. He lived with his family on the Isle of Skye, an island off the coast of Scotland.

One morning Donald went skipping across the moor. He was careful not to step on hillocks, for that is where fairies live. And who knows what mischief fairies might do one?

Under his arm Donald carried his chanter. He was on his way to Mister MacSkirl's house for his bagpipe lesson.

Donald did not have a bagpipe of his own. But Mister MacSkirl had promised to loan Donald a set of bagpipes for the competition tomorrow.

There was to be a great celebration in honor of the MacLeod chief's birthday. The people would gather at Dunvegan Castle for feasting and games. There would be a piping contest, and the winner would receive the title of Piper to the Chief. Just thinking about that made Donald excited.

Suddenly the boy stopped, grabbed off his cap, and threw it at a swirl of dust on the road. Dust eddies are made by the fairies moving. If you throw your cap or your left shoe at them, the fairies have to drop anything they might be stealing.

Donald watched intently, but nothing dropped out of the cloud of dust. He picked up his cap and skipped on.

Mister MacSkirl was digging peat near his cottage when Donald got there.

"Here, boy," he called gruffly, "make yourself useful and earn your lesson."

"Yes, sir," answered Donald. He laid his chanter down carefully, then he helped stack the clumps of peat neatly.

On the Isle of Skye, where Donald lived, the ground is very rocky and trees do not grow well. Instead of using wood for their fires, people burn peat, which is something like earth and something like coal. It makes a smoky fire, but nobody minds.

Donald worked hard. Even so, it was a long time before MacSkirl stopped.

"Fill the creel with peat, Donald, and come along," he finally said.

MacSkirl led the way into the cottage and poured himself a cup of hot broth. He did not offer any to Donald, so the boy helped himself to a drink of water from the pail in the corner. MacSkirl was a mean man. But he was a good piper, and—oh!—Donald did want to be a good piper, too.

"Well, let's hear it," MacSkirl said, leaning back in his chair.

Donald picked up his chanter and played the tune that he had been practicing that week. When he stopped, his teacher did not say anything. Donald waited anxiously while MacSkirl got up and lifted his bagpipe from the peg.

Donald wiped his hands carefully on his kilt and took the pipes. He tucked the bag under his arm, put the drones over his shoulder, and blew into the blowpipe so that air filled the bag, making it fat and firm under his arm.

Then Donald played the tune again. And then he played another tune, and another. His eyes got big and his cheeks got red and his fingers flew over the holes in the chanter. How he loved the music of the bagpipe! He stamped one foot in time with the music until the very walls shook and startled birds flew out of the thatched roof.

"Tomorrow," Donald thought, "tomorrow I will

pipe in the competition. There will be banners flying and people cheering, and I will stand among the other pipers of the clan. How proud my family will be! How excited—"

Suddenly Donald became aware that MacSkirl was glaring at him. He quickly stopped piping and asked, "What did I do wrong, sir?"

Now, MacSkirl had just realized that Donald played the pipes better than he himself could do! This made him angry. To himself he thought, "If Donald pipes tomorrow, he may win the contest instead of me."

Aloud, MacSkirl said, "I was just thinking how disappointed you'll be, Donald, but I don't have any pipes to loan you for tomorrow."

Donald held tight to the bagpipe under his arm and cried, "Oh, Mister MacSkirl, you promised—"

"I know, I know," said MacSkirl crossly, "but I just didn't get around to fixing my old bagpipe for you, so that's that."

He took his pipes away from Donald and turned his back on the boy. Mean as he was, it bothered him to see how close to tears Donald was. Donald stood there a moment, pleading silently, but MacSkirl did not turn around.

Donald picked up his chanter, put his bonnet on his head, and silently let himself out the door. Head hanging, he stumbled down the road.

"He promised, he promised," Donald said over and over to himself.

Suddenly there was a loud crash of thunder, and a gust of wind blew cold on his neck. Donald raised his head and noticed that it had become very dark. He started to run, but just then the rain came pouring down.

Soon it was raining so hard that Donald could hardly see the road. He stopped. The bridge over the little river was around here somewhere. There was no railing on the bridge. It would be easy to—

Just then Donald heard a cry and a splash ahead of him. He ran forward, and in a flash of lightning he saw a little old woman struggling in the water under the bridge.

Donald scrambled down the bank, caught hold of her cloak, and hauled the old woman up to safety.

"Are you all right?" he cried.

"Oh, yes, yes, indeed! And thank you very much."

She stood there, bobbing her head and smiling at him through the rain. "And how are you?" she asked politely, folding her hands in front of her, and Donald noticed what a tiny old lady she was.

"Oh, well, fine—" Donald mumbled, "except that I'm wet, of course."

"My goodness, you are wet! How did that happen?"

Donald stared at her in surprise. "It's raining," he said.

"Why, so it is!" the old lady exclaimed. "Don't stand there gabbing. Come in where it's dry."

She grabbed the boy by his hand and scurried across the moor, pulling him with her.

Donald could not see a thing, it was so dark and rainy. All that he could do was cling to the strange little old lady's hand and run to keep up with her.

"Here we are!" she cried. And suddenly there was a door in front of them. She pushed it open, drew Donald in, and slammed the door against the storm.

Donald stood there, panting, and brushed the wet hair out of his eyes.

"Now for some nice, hot barley broth," said the little old lady.

As she put the kettle on the fire, Donald looked at her curiously. She certainly was a funny little lady. She was no bigger than he, with a wide smile, a very large nose, rosy cheeks, and eyes that crinkled almost shut when she smiled. She had wispy white hair and was dressed all in green.

All in green! Why, maybe she was a fairy!

Donald quickly stuck his knife in the door as a magic charm against being kept prisoner. He looked toward the little old lady to see if she had seen him. He didn't want to hurt her feelings.

She was watching him and laughing. "Yes," she nodded, "I'm one of the 'good people,' young man, but I won't do you any mischief. You did me a good turn, and I won't forget it."

She beamed at Donald and he smiled back. "Yes, indeedy, a very kind deed it was, pulling me out of the wet the way you did. I'm grateful to you and—"

"Excuse me, ma'am," Donald interrupted, "but the broth is boiling over into the fire."

"Ohhhh!" the fairy said, whirling to pull the kettle away from the heat. "I do that every time," she confessed, chuckling.

Then while she poured the broth, Donald pulled up a bench to the fireplace so that their clothes could dry.

"Isn't this cozy?" said the fairy, swinging her feet. "But you're not very happy," she added, cocking her head on one side to peer into Donald's face.

"Yes, I am," he declared stoutly.

"No, you're not," the fairy insisted.

A tear ran down Donald's cheek and splashed into his cup. "I wanted to pipe in the games tomorrow, but

I don't have a bagpipe," he explained.

"I have a bagpipe," said the fairy.

"Are you going to play tomorrow?" asked Donald.

But the fairy had already skipped across the room and had her head buried in a big chest in the corner. She was mumbling to herself, "I'm quite sure I have a bagpipe here somewhere."

As she searched through the chest, the fairy tossed things over her shoulder—
a rabbit skin, a bird's nest,
  a clump of peat, a tweed vest,
    some oat cakes, a birch broom,
      some seashells, a broken loom,
      one green stocking ("I wondered where that was"),
      and then ("Oh, goody!") a bagpipe.

The fairy waded through the things on the floor, sat down beside Donald again, and handed him the bagpipe.

"How do you like that?" she inquired.

The bag was sturdy sheepskin and the pipes were wood, beautifully carved, with bands of silver and ivory.

"It's the handsomest set of pipes I've ever seen," Donald answered.

"You may keep it," said the fairy. "It will be your very own bagpipe, but it can be played only by you."

"Oh . . ." cried Donald, but before he could say more, the strange little lady said, "Your clothes are dry. You'd better go home, now."

She pulled Donald across the floor, handed him his knife, and pushed him out the door.

"Goodbye," called Donald as the door shut behind him. "I forgot that fairies don't like to be thanked."

He looked at his new bagpipe with delight. Hugging it tightly in his arms, he started for home.

The next morning Donald was up early, urging his family to hurry. It was the day for the gathering at Dunvegan Castle. Right after breakfast, Donald, his little sister, and his mother and father set off across the moor.

When the MacCrimmons arrived, the great fires were already roaring. Huge chunks of meat were roasting. All the clansmen had come with something for the feast—strings of fish, fresh-baked bread and cakes and scones, honey and jam. Donald felt hungry just looking at all the good things to eat.

In the harbor by the castle many boats came, bringing visitors. Across the road from the castle was a big open field where the games were already starting.

Donald munched on this and that while he wandered around the field, watching everything. All day there was racing and wrestling and caber tossing and hammer throwing.

Then late in the afternoon, Mister MacKenzie—who had been chosen because he had the loudest voice—shouted, "Pipers! Get ready!" and the contest Donald had waited for began.

Throwing the Hammer

Piper MacClure was first. Donald would be last, after O'Neil from Ireland and Mister MacSkirl.

Donald waited happily, enjoying the music. He did not notice MacSkirl a few steps away. The old man stared at the boy from underneath his bushy eyebrows. He had a good set of pipes himself, but Donald's pipes were the best he had ever seen.

Finally Mister MacSkirl spoke to Donald. "I'm sorry that I didn't fix up my old pipes for you," he said.

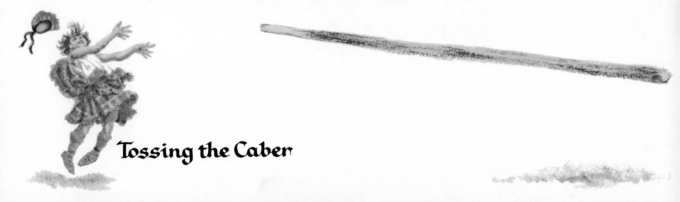

Tossing the Caber

"Oh, that's all right, sir," said Donald happily. "I have a bagpipe of my own now."

"So I see. But it's not a very good one. I'll tell you what I'll do, my boy, I'll trade with you."

And what did MacSkirl do then but jerk Donald's pipes from him and shove his own bagpipe at the boy. Then off he started. Of course MacSkirl had not the

least idea of how Donald had come by his bagpipe—he only wanted it for himself.

Donald tried to race after the man. "No, no!" he called. "Please, Mister MacSkirl, I don't want to trade."

Just then MacSkirl's name was called, and he marched out on the field, leaving Donald weeping with anger.

Suddenly the boy heard such a strange noise that he stopped crying. What could it be? MacSkirl was playing. But it didn't sound like bagpipe music, it sounded like a cat fight.

There were squeals, shrieks, and gurgles. The bagpipe was wheezing and gasping like a sick cow. MacSkirl's fingers were slurring every hoarse note.

At first the crowd listened in surprised silence. Then someone tittered and someone else giggled. And in a moment, the whole crowd was rocking with laughter.

MacSkirl was bewildered. The pipes fell from his shaking hands. He pulled his bonnet down over his ears and fled.

Donald watched in amazement. Then he heard his own name called, "Donald MacCrimmon!" He ran out on the field, picked up his pipes, tucked them lovingly under his arm, and puffing out his cheeks, began to play.

The laughter and hooting died as the people turned to listen to Donald. His music was as slow and sad and lonely as a single gull wheeling in a bleak sky.

The crowd grew very quiet as Donald paced slowly up and down and the music sang of hardship and loneliness and disappointment. It made the listeners think of the cold wind sweeping over the moor and the gray waves rolling against the rocks.

Then Donald quickened his step, and the people lifted their heads as his music changed. It rolled out proud and glad, proud of the very hardness of life because it offered a challenge to overcome. People began to tap their feet, to nod and smile. This music made them proud of their beautiful Isle of Skye, proud of being Scotsmen, proud of belonging to the MacLeod clan. The music swelled until everyone could feel it going through him, and the ground trembled with the warm, stirring tune.

Then Donald stopped.

For a minute there was silence and Donald thought, "No one liked it. But I know I played well."

He lifted his chin proudly and started to march off the field.

As if there had been a signal, the crowd came to life with a roar. People rushed out on the field. Donald felt himself siezed by friendly hands. He was lifted up on someone's shoulder and carried around the field. People cheered and screamed and stamped their feet. Bonnets flew into the air.

Finally Donald was set down on his own feet in front of the MacLeod chief. The tall old man shook the boy's hand and said solemnly, "Donald MacCrimmon, that was the greatest piping I have ever heard. I am proud to call you Piper to the Chief."

And then Donald's parents were beside him. His father clapped him proudly on the shoulder, his mother hugged him, and his little sister jumped up and down with excitement.

Then there was feasting and drinking of toasts, and Donald had to play for dancing as the long, happy day led into a long, happy night. And the happiest person in all that celebration was Donald McCrimmon, Piper to the Chief.

Gerry and George Armstrong

The idea for the story of *The Magic Bagpipe* took form while Gerry and George Armstrong were spending a honeymoon vacation on the Isle of Skye in 1954. There they visited Dunvegan Castle and had tea as the guests of Dame Flora MacLeod, the twenty-sixth Chief of the Clan.

Today the Armstrongs have two daughters, Becky and Jenny, and make their home in Wilmette, Illinois. They share the hobby of folk music and have given concerts and recorded two LP albums of American and British folk songs. Music from Scotland has special meaning for George because he learned as a boy to play the bagpipe. He has played in bands before Queen Elizabeth and General Eisenhower.

The possibility of combining their interests in music and Scotland to make a children's book intrigued the Armstrongs. And so Gerry wrote *The Magic Bagpipe* and George contributed the handsome illustrations. He is by profession an artist, specializing in school histories and encyclopedias. The article and accompanying illustrations for Scottish tartan in the *Encyclopaedia Britannica* are his work.

The calligraphy for *The Magic Bagpipe* was done by Wm. A. Norman.

MacCrimmon's Sweetheart

Air adapted from the pibroch   Words by Gerry & George Armstrong

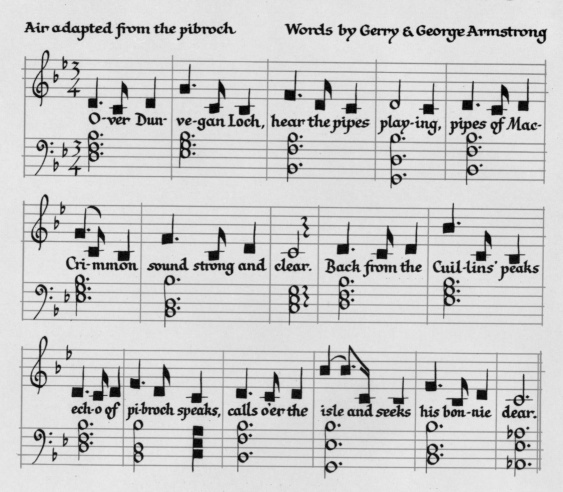

O-ver Dun- ve-gan Loch, hear the pipes play-ing, pipes of Mac-Cri-mmon sound strong and clear. Back from the Cuil-lins' peaks ech-o of pi-broch speaks, calls o'er the isle and seeks his bon-nie dear.

Bonnie the isle, with its plaidie of heather,
Ribboned with sparkling, silvery streams;
Beauty of bird on wing, mystery of fairy ring,
Murmur of sea waves sing, filling my dreams.

Dunvegan Loch

🏰 Dunvegan Castle

Isle of Skye

Cuillin Hills